D1495812

KC's Christmas Discovery

WRITTEN BY

Estelle H. Herndon

ILLUSTRATED BY

Samantha Bell

Paperback ISBN-13: 978-1-948026-50-5
Digital ISBN-13: 978-1-948026-51-2
Hardcover ISBN-13: 978-1-948026-52-9

Published by TMP Books, 3 Central Plaza Ste 307, Rome, GA 30161
www.TMPBooks.com
Editorial Assistant: Carrie Leeth

Published in the United States of America.

Dedication

In Loving Memory
Karen Rebecca Clifton
October 14, 1938 – October 3, 2017

And Honoring
Braxton,
who helped write this book.

KC is a curious little mouse
Who lives with her family in the Herndon house.

She is tiny and gray, with little fuzzy ears
that let her know when anyone nears.

One night when KC was fast asleep
Loud noises startled her from the bed with a leap!

She scurried and hurried without making a sound,
Toward the music and laughter
And much more she soon found.

As KC peeked from the shadows that night
Popa's voice boomed with great might.

"Come everyone, come and see,
Our beautiful and special Christmas tree!"

KC sneaked closer so that she might see
This thing he called a Christmas Tree.

Twinkling and shiny,
the tree was all aglow.
Lights from every corner
Way up high
And even way down low.

KC stretched and stretched,
but she still couldn't see
What was on the very top of that
Christmas tree.

But, oh, what a glorious sight!

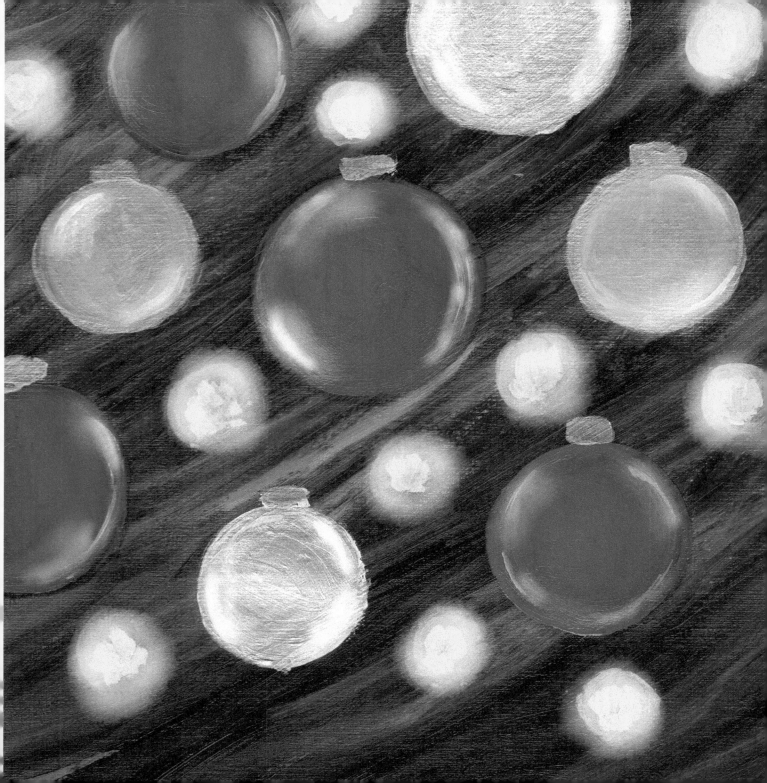

Red and green, silver and gold
Lights and ornaments, some new and some old,
All different shapes and none the same size,
Each one offering its own little surprise.

Glitzy and glowing putting on a big show
KC's eyes move to and fro
From the bottom of the tree up to the very top
Then something caught her eye and she had to stop.

KC moved closer, looking at the round ball.

Perched on the end, she hoped it wouldn't fall.

She smiled and the mouse on the ball smiled, too.

KC laughed at something so new.

She smiled again, just to see.

"Could that mouse on the ball

really be me?"

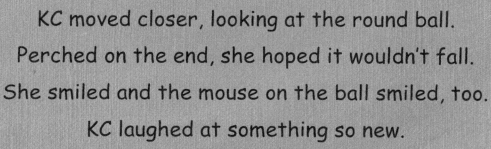
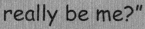

Then she spied something so big and so bright
Shining from way high on the tree
KC inched even closer, just so she could see.

Peeking through limbs and branches of the tree,
The shape twinkled and sparkled with light
Dazzling as it could be.

The tree towered over her, but finally she could see
The whole shimmering light at the top of the tree.

Can you guess what KC saw that night
That filled her with such pure delight?

A Star!
A shining star sat on top of that tree
A Star so wonderful
KC just had to see!

KC hurried up that tree
Looking as far as she could see,
Sitting in front of the beautiful star,
It shined even brighter
than it did from afar!

Sitting on that tree, eyes opened wide
KC felt all mushy inside.
The tree and the lights and the star up above
And the family below made her heart
Swell with great love.

Music floated through the air
As they sang and danced with great flair.

As KC danced her way down the tree,
She listened to the words they sang
with joy and glee.

Happy Birthday, Jesus!
They sang from their heart,
In pure harmony even from the start.

Happy Birthday, Jesus!

Hiding behind the colorful presents and bows,
She listened to what Nana had to say:
"Jesus is the only way.

Just ask Him into your heart.
He forgives you of your sins and you become a part

Of this Joyful, Happy Day.
Jesus is the only way!"

As KC raced back up that Christmas tree
JOY grew in her heart,
And made her want to be a part
Of celebrating
Jesus' birthday!

KC wanted to know Jesus, too!
But what should she do?

KC thought about Jesus as she climbed toward the star
Thinking of all she'd heard that night so far.
The story that they read and the songs
they'd sung too,
Helped KC to know that
Jesus is true!

Right then and there,
on the branch of that Christmas tree.
KC asked Jesus to come into her heart
to live there forever and never depart.

Whispering to Jesus, she said,
"Thank you, Jesus, for hearing my prayer too.
Thank you for forgiving me!
Jesus, I love you!"

KC ran down the tree and began jumping for joy,
Singing and dancing, looking like a little toy.

They were all singing and dancing with such glee,
Joining young and old, tall and small,
Celebrating Jesus' birthday.
Now THIS was KC's call.

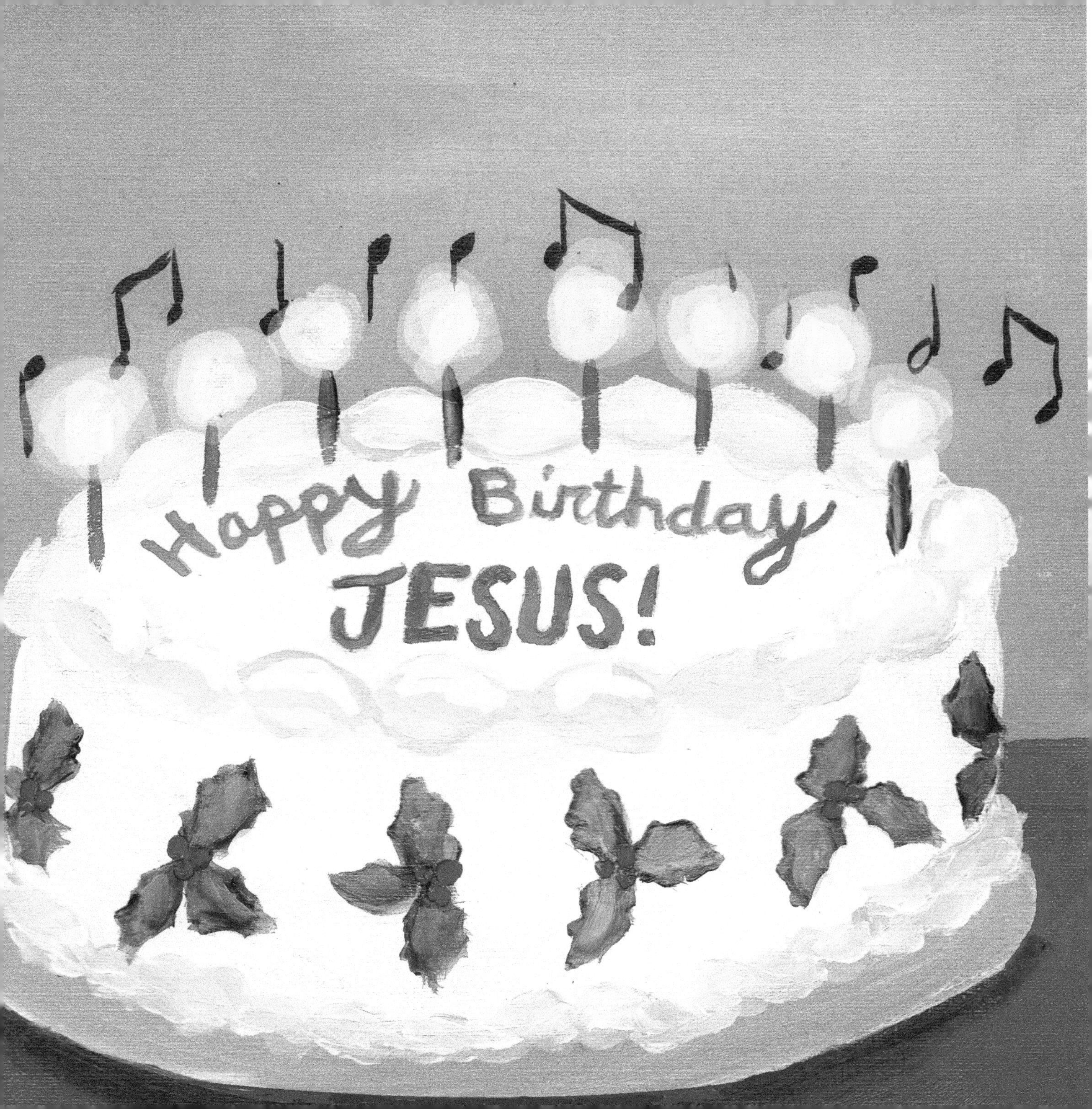
Happy Birthday
JESUS!

The Real Christmas Story

Now in those days a decree went out from Caesar Augustus, that a census be taken of all the inhabited earth. This was the first census taken while Quirinius was governor of Syria. And everyone was on his way to register for the census, each to his own city. Joseph also went up from Galilee, from the city of Nazareth, to Judea, to the city of David which is called Bethlehem, because he was of the house and family of David, in order to register along with Mary, who was engaged to him, and was with child. While they were there, the days were completed for her to give birth. And she gave birth to her firstborn son; and she wrapped Him in cloths, and laid Him in a manger, because there was no room for them in the inn.

In the same region there were some shepherds staying out in the fields and keeping watch over their flock by night. And an angel of the Lord suddenly stood before them, and the glory of the Lord shone around them; and they were terribly frightened. But the angel said to them, "Do not be afraid; for behold, I bring you good news of great joy which will be for all the people; for today in the city of David there has been born for you a Savior, who is Christ the Lord. This will be a sign for you: you will find a baby wrapped in cloths and lying in a manger."

(continued on next page)

(continued from previous page)

And suddenly there appeared with the angel a multitude of the heavenly host praising God and saying,

"Glory to God in the highest,
And on earth peace among men with whom He is pleased."

When the angels had gone away from them into heaven, the shepherds began saying to one another, "Let us go straight to Bethlehem then, and see this thing that has happened which the Lord has made known to us." So they came in a hurry and found their way to Mary and Joseph, and the baby as He lay in the manger. When they had seen this, they made known the statement which had been told them about this Child. And all who heard it wondered at the things which were told them by the shepherds. But Mary treasured all these things, pondering them in her heart. The shepherds went back, glorifying and praising God for all that they had heard and seen, just as had been told them.

Luke 2: 1-20
New American Standard Bible

Note from the Author

When people commit their lives to Our Lord Jesus, something amazing happens to them, and that's exactly what happened to me.

I am forever His. I have been purchased; His Spirit is my receipt. I am a child of the King. Sharing Jesus with children is one of my greatest desires.

My sincere hope is that when children learn of KC's Christmas Discovery, they will want to know Jesus and will come to know Him like I know Him. I have had the greatest honor to be called His child, and my prayer is that each child will accept Jesus as their own personal Lord and Savior. On the next page, I've shared some of my favorite Bible verses to share with children.

The story of KC honors a dear friend, Karen Clifton, who now resides in her new home with our Lord. My mind visualizes Karen playing the piano or organ, enjoying every moment of each melody. Cancer did not win her life. The Lord called her home to be with Him. She is His spokesperson, using her gift of music. I see her as an angel on the keyboard.

Dear Parents, Grandparents, Friends,

Jesus loves us. He desires to have a personal relationship with each of us, and with each member of our family. He wants to give you a life full of joy and purpose.

We each have a past. He can walk into those places, wipe the slate clean, and give each one of us a new beginning, if we ask Him in.

We need a friend Who knows the best and worst about us. Yet He sees the best we can be with Him.

He holds our future in His hands. He has plans for good and not for evil for us. He hears our prayers and listens, never sleeping, no matter when or where we pray.

If you want a personal relationship with Jesus, just ask Him into your heart, your life. Let Him know you believe He died for you forever.

Tell Him you want to receive this free gift He offers you, that you want Him to be Lord and Savior of your life, and that you want to spend eternity (forever) with Him.

He waits patiently for you. He loves you that much.

Love,
Essie

Some of the Author's Favorite Bible Verses

Children, obey your parents in the Lord, for this is right. Honor your father and mother (which is the first commandment with a promise), so that it may be well with you, and that you may live long on the earth.   **Ephesians 6: 1-3**

Therefore be imitators of God, as beloved children; and walk in love, just as Christ also loved you and gave Himself up for us, an offering and a sacrifice to God as a fragrant aroma. **Ephesians 5: 1-2**

Little children, let us not love with word or with tongue, but in deed and truth.   **1 John 3:18**

Come, you children, listen to me;
I will teach you the fear of the Lord.
Who is the man who desires life
And loves length of days that he may see good?
Keep your tongue from evil
And your lips from speaking deceit.
Depart from evil and do good;
Seek peace and pursue it.   **Psalm 34: 11-14**

Whoever receives one child like this in My name receives Me.   **Mark 9:37a**

Command your children to obey carefully all the words of this law. They are not just idle words for you—they are your life.   **Deuteronomy 32: 46b-47 (NIV)**

For the Son of Man has come to seek and to save that which was lost.   **Luke 19:10**

His [Jesus'] name will be called Wonderful Counselor, Mighty God, Eternal Father, Prince of Peace.   **Isaiah 9:6**

But Jesus said, "Let the children alone, and do not hinder them from coming to Me because the kingdom of Heaven belongs to such as these."

                                            Matthew 19:14

About the Author

Estelle "Essie" H. Herndon, is a Christ Follower, wife, mother, grandmother, great-grandmother and prayer warrior. She has worked alongside her husband, Robert, as his paralegal for over forty-seven years.

Essie is active in her church. She teaches with her husband in Bible studies and leading small groups, helping with Women's Ministries and Grief Ministries, from youth to young married adults.

She is also active in her community, having served on various boards over the years.

Her family and friends are her hobbies. She and husband Robert enjoy traveling which has included Georgia football games.

She truly tries to please God in her daily activities, always remembering where she has been in her past and how God has worked in her life for His Honor. She lives in Georgia.

Essie's nonfiction book, ***Finding His Strength***, released in 2017.

Loving life. Free in HIS strength!

Thank you
for reading our books!

Look for other books published by

www.TMPBooks.com

*If you enjoyed this book,
a review is greatly appreciated!*